CARNIVAL IN PARIS

Carnival in Paris

Library of Congress Control Number. 2025

(For performance or permission requests, please contact Author at publishingchalet@gmail.com)

ISBN:.....(e-book) *979-8-9925199-5-2*
ISBN (softback) *979-8-9925199-6-9*
ISBN (hardback) *979-8-9925199-4-5*
Publisher's Cataloging-in-Publication Dataprovided by Five Rainbows Cataloging ServicesNames:Piccolo,J. Renee,author.Title:Carnival in Paris/J. Renee Piccolo.Description:Pompano Beach, FL:Publishing Chalet,2026. | Summary:An epic carnivalpoem fromParis France to New York and back!Identifiers: ISBN979-8-9925199-6-9(paperback) | ISBN979-8-9925199-5-2(hardcover)Subjects: LCSH:Poetry.|Short stories. |CYAC:Young adult poetry. |Young adult fiction. |Carnivals--Fiction.|Family life--Fiction|BISAC:YOUNG ADULT FICTION / Poetry. |YOUNGADULT FICTION / Performing Arts / General. |YOUNG ADULT FICTION / Places / Europe.|YOUNG ADULT FICTION / Places / United States.Classification: LCCPZ7.1.P53 Car 2026(print) | DDC[Fic]--dc23

Carnival in Paris

Poem by,

J. Renee Piccolo

Publishing Chalet, USA

Dedication

Has life ever felt like a merry-go-round? Happy one minute, then let down. Sometimes feeling like a show pony. Put on your beret for an epic carnival poem from Paris France to New York and back!

To those who think life is easier as a clown. To those who left, and the ones who stuck around.

Enjoy the ride.

Admit one!

Glossary

Mr. Claude Choo – *carnival dad*

Mrs. Claudette Choo - *carnival mom*

Jon-Claude Phillipe Choo – *carnival son*

Penelope Choo – *carnival wife*

Pinky le' Poo - *carnival fish*

Miss. Amelia – *teacher / mime*

Mr. Carnie Cahoots – *co-worker / friend*

Carnie's, Yuti and Tuti – *carnival friends*

Clown Jules / Clown Jubilee – *classmates*

Mr. Babsy - *zookeeper*

Penny Novelty Choo – *carnival baby*

Table of Contents

Part One..... The Little Tent Page 3

Part Two..... The Big Tent Page 13

Part Three.... The Stunt Page 36

Part Four..... The Last Show Page 64

“Knock knock…”

“Who’s there?”

“A clown…”

“A clown who?

“Who loves you.”

Part One:

The Little Tent

In the summer of 1992, lived a family of carnival employees in Paris, France.

Address: train station, bench twenty-two - at the *Gare de Lyon*. A place of beautiful architecture, rich culture, standard poodles too.

It all started when two people accidentally head-butted on their way to work.

"Hello *bonjour, comment' talle' vous*?" asked Mr. Claude in French, a local mechanical engineer at the town fair.

"I'm fine, and you..." said Mrs. Claudette, a fine arts major, whose passion is painting clowns.

"Nice to meet you... let me get that for you," he said, reaching down as her travel pass dropped to the ground, mentioning, "trains are wonderful."

"Oh, yes, I think so too! I could practically live in one," she replied.

His eyes went extra wide, then he humored her, "Would you believe my last name is Choo."

"I'll call you Choo-Choo!" she joked, making it sound fancy.

It was there, in an opulent dining room, the future Mr. and Mrs. Claude and Claudette Choo, wined and dined at *Le Train Bleu* where they woo each other over a crepe for two.

Without hesitation, she fell head over heels in love, looking down to notice his big toe poking through worn-out shoes.

In a long-thrifted dress and luxury handbag, she thought to herself, "That'll do!"

He appeared to be a malnourished man, who wore ripped slender pants held up by elastic bands.

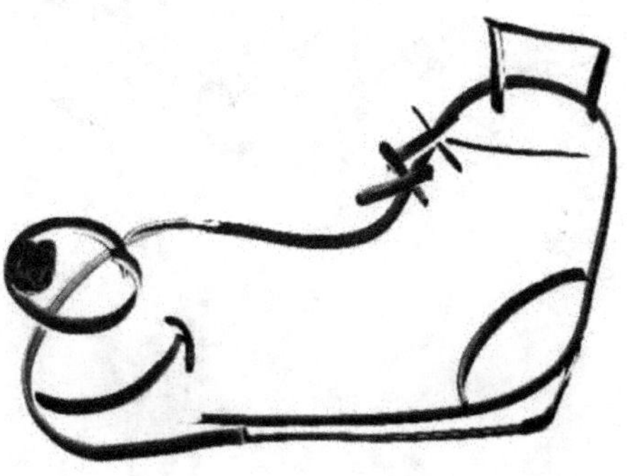

“All you need is love,” Mrs. Claudette told him, as the string of her hearts-balloon pulled away to the moon.

What seemed unfair was all he knew. Sharing a philosophy, she held true, reminding him, “Life is a gift, buy a balloon or bouquet to celebrate the day.”

Him... the calculated brains; her... beyond witty, with captivating beauty.

Arriving home to the station after a day of work, she elegantly waits for him, spraying perfume as potpourri.

"*Mon' Cherie*, you look so lovely!"

"*Merci*, thank you," she replied flattered. "May I exchange your ticket to one way? Would you stay with me under these vaulted ceilings?" he asked wishing to not part ways.

A silence filled the rose-colored air, unsure what to say. Gazing at crooked, unaligned teeth with two brackets, she answered, “Heck, what’s one more day; let’s toast over a bottle of cabernet.”

Day turned to dark, a beautiful night for a stroll in the park. Black and white swans fill the pond of water lilies.

Pretty as a picture, they held hands as the sidewalk lights flicker. An evening rendezvous, for the future Mr. and Mrs. Choo.

It wasn't long after dating, when Mr. Claude said, "Claudette, I have something to tell you..."

Difficulty in finding the right words, the warm-hearted woman said, "Well, go ahead, we don't have all day to waste."

Stumbling to speak, sweating from his head to his feet, he expressed, "*Mademoiselle,* I think... I love you. I'm sorry if it's too soon."

Out for a joy ride, they spent February to June - train hopping.

A life of love and laughter she would perceive, without a hitch, Mrs. Claudette soon conceived. In secret, they traveled to a small chapel to make it official, at the *Sainte-Chapelle*. Located at the *Boulevard du Palais or* known as Boulevard of the Palace- a holy crystal house.

Nine months later, Mrs. Claudette-Choo left a note, 'Went to the store... will be back around four o'clock.'

On the list with only a pocketful of cents: flowers, a fresh baguette, and vegetable florets; unexpectedly, going into labor on aisle two with Jon-Claude Phillipe Choo.

Part Two:

The Big Tent

Over the years as their boy grew, they learned to make do. Finding an outdated, rigidity-raggedy-flippity-flappity-clickity-clackity-wobbly-dobbly, train cabin to move into.

"All aboard!" shouts the attendant.

A lanky baby, perfectly-imperfect for parents of little Choo. Born unusual, and yet unique with two left feet at thirty inches. He was quite the sight, crisscrossing one foot in front of the other to walk a straight line.

On most days, Jon-Claude Phillipe Choo was homeschooled at the 't-station' learning the bare minimum. For lunch- moldy snacks, a pack of bubble chew, and a can of carbonated syrup.

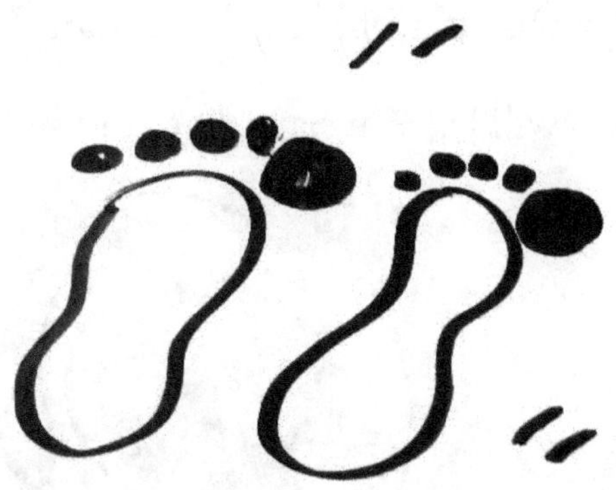

When sitting in front of the television, it did not matter where the train was headed... Timbuktu or Kalamazoo.

"Alright son, big news! It's time you go to clown school. You can't just sit here all day and wither away, it's unhealthy for your disability."

His mother interrupts, "Well, we shall wait until next year. For now, bring him with you to work at the fair for life lessons."

"A wise plan for my little man. In the morning, we will leave at 5am," he told his wife.

Before sunrise, they hopped trains four blocks to the nearest town's carnival, already excited for the pony show.

The first day was how to win. Mr. Claude Choo shared, "Listen here, never let anyone steal your joy," he continued, "even these horses lose many times, and they never stop trying. Failure is not the last run."

Day two fixing the mechanical dunk tank, they switch booths to win a gift.

"Press your luck, catch a duck," hollered a man.

"I'm hoping for a real pet, sir," Jon-Claude said, then left to the next stand.

After a few games they skipped out of the park to the grand station, when carnie siblings, Yuti and Tuti, invite Jon-Claude Phillipe Choo over, yelling, "Take a risk, win a fish!"

Stopping for more fun, he couldn't resist, "Dad, can we?"

"Toss the ball in the middle, this one's on me," said the carnival man.

"Yay, I did it! I won the prize," he shouted.

"A pet friend, you got your wish!" replied his father, who says, "we shall also buy a balloon for your mother."

As they pass the last stand to exit the park, a lady calls out, "Over here! Win something you don't have to flush in the morning!"

"Ha, we're okay mam," Mr. Claude told her as they made their back to the city. Stopping for a moment, his father said, "I must use the *loo*; wait here and run if you hear *gardyloo*! They may be tossing pails over the rails."

"No worries. I will be admiring the jugglers, and store windows selling chandeliers."

At home, Jon-Claude surprised his mother with a balloon attached to a box with a sweet treat and wrapped in a bow. Behind his back was the new Parisian pet in hand.

“Look what I won! A bright neon fish.”

“That’s great, son! Have you picked out a name?”

“Pinky le’ Poo!”

“Fabulous! Take it everywhere with you, an early responsibility,” she replied, placing the gift on a tiny chair. “Hmm... and a name for my pet rock...” she pondered.

“It’s a truffle to eat, not a rock,” chuckled Jon Claude Phillipe Choo.

A new week, another lesson ensued risking their lives for nickels and dimes. Imperative to stay on track, his father insists he always wears running shoes, "Don't end up like this old vintage pair, tripping and stumbling over my feet," he would say.

"Woah, aah," Jon-Claude muttered with a big splash.

"Lookout, your footing!" shouted Mr. Claude, "be careful not to end up in a ring-worm puddle with those rubbery things you're wearing."

"Phew, close call! Sorry pops."

There is no time to slow down, like a merry-go-round, progress was to keep moving.

"Life is a series of Merry's, you're well prepared for what's ahead; it's nothing to dread," said Mr. Claude to his Mini-Choo.

They headed home to decompress, when a man rode by on his horse, almost slipping.

"Perfect timing," said Mr. Claude, "when we fall we get back up, because we're steadfast humans like pure-bred stallions. Someday, just like your mom's art, you too, will win an award ribbon."

"How will I?" asked Jon-Claude.

"I'm saying not to worry... you're already doing trophy laps on the right path."

Week three quickly approaches with speed. Mrs. Claudette made breakfast when coaching him, "Today, play it smart on the go-karts. Don't rush to red to get ahead; the outcome is the same."

"Sounds great! Pinky le' Poo will go too! I'm sure she's tired of her one by one," he told his mother.

"Okay, stay hydrated. Drink plenty of water and make sure your fish doesn't drown. Don't forget to refill the tank," reminding him of delicate life.

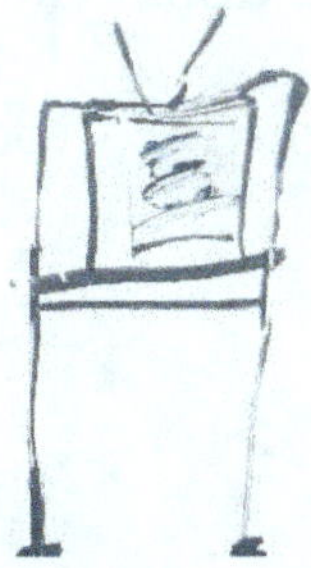

Temperatures in the mid-nineties cause them to be thirsty, when his *père* shared, "I'll explain my lemonade theory while we order one. What do you say?"

"Oh, sounds delicious, may we?!"

Mr. Claude handed the worker $4.75 asking for extra sweetness, until the carnie said, "I'm going to need a bit more, you have another twenty-five cents for added sugar?"

So, he reached in his pocket to give him a five-dollar bill, and told his little one, "Give me high-five – today, we make it count."

"A harsh squeeze in a cup, drink up, the best is at the bottom," he promised, "just be careful of an addiction."

"Oh, yay, I always have so much fun with you!" said Jon-Claude Phillipe Choo.

They carry on after a lovely day, stopping at a local bakery for the finest pastries. Never to forget his mères favorite - raspberry sachet.

At the train cabin, they arrive to a smorgasbord of carnival food with a nutritional side dish of *le' cordon blue.*

After dinner, Mr. Claude-Choo tried to rest, doodling on paper he softly said to his still hyper son, "You know this train is a circus, let me relax before the next crappy show."

Never moody - unwinding with a glass of Pinot.

In the middle of the night, his beeper went off. He assumed the fairgrounds owner had made a mistake.

Dialing him back, he asked, "Why so late?"

"Can you be here by eight in the morning? The big wheel and rides stopped operating. Possibly struck by lightning."

Mr. Claude Choo knew exactly what to do. Soon, he taught his growing boy lesson four - how to settle a score with the land's slumlord. Instructing how to necessarily walk a tight rope to balance on the beam of light through life.

Arriving to the carnival early, he called the head honcho to make a deal he couldn't refuse.

"Hey buddy, I'm low on funds and need some money to turn my lights on. If you write me a paycheck in advance, you will once again make steady income."

So, he hung up the mobile phone, reassembled the lines and tested the wires with his pride and joy, his intuitive boy.

"Testing 1-2"

"Testing 3-4"

"Testing 1-2-3-4"

"Testing 4-3-2-1," repeated Mr. Claude, going back and forth on the machines.

"Hmm... are we adding or counting? asked Jon Claude.

"I must tweak and manipulate it to once again function properly, like they say... 'if there's a will, there is a way.' And that's how you fix the tilt-n-twist."

Taking time off to re-coup, week five was overdue. Mrs. Claudette awakes Jon-Claude Phillipe Choo and his father, who've overslept to sounds of a rainstorm.

"Hurry, so you don't miss the trolley!" she said with an echo.

In the rusty train cabin, Mr. Claude gathered his tools, blow horn, and umbrella handing them to Jon-Claude, he said, "Here, hold this too."

It was all very heavy when he thought to himself, "Is this real life. I must gain ten pounds."

For two weeks, he overate, causing him to have a terrible stomachache. Eventually, ending up in a tailor's studio fitted for large suspenders.

“Now what?” he asked, “I can lift this, but can’t carry my own weight.”

“It was the very large funnel cake on your plate,” warned Mr. Claude, “good news though, you’ll make a wonderful clown, don’t frown.”

“Okay, Pops, we don’t have much, so I’ll be the best in town.”

That year standing in front of the mirror, he practiced jokes and quirky facial expressions with his fan club manager, Pinky le’ Poo.

Jon-Claude Phillipe Choo shares joy and humor with others, often giving out balloons with his mother; one of his favorite things to do.

"Excuse me, *monsieur*, do you know the way to clown school?" he asked a random civilian.

"Oh dear, pardon our French," said his mother, the boy is confused."

"It's alright, I no longer feel blue," replied the man, who was quite flabbergasted. "Thank you for making my day better. Whoops, did I toot," he said brazenly.

"Choo-Choo!!" Jon-Claude joked.

"Don't laugh at him sweetie; wherever you may be, let your wind free. We should be going now, your father is waiting for us," his mother assured him. "Nice to meet you sir, farewell!"

"Same to you, *Madame, adieu*!"

Later that day, very excited to see animals roam freely, he raced to put on unmatched socks and a visor with a fan on top. Behind on time, Mr. Claude said, "If we're late for the zoo, you will miss the gorillas smile at you."

They quickly arrived along with Pinky le' Poo. But when the lion noticed a fish, he instinctively roars so loud that Jon-Claude's hair blew wildly into the air. Just then, he said, "Hey *père*, um... I think I'm ready for clown school."

"Ha, you're like me, undoubtedly cuckoo."

Part Three:

The Stunt

That night, Jon-Claude Phillipe Choo packed a small backpack for the airport, thinking, 'I can't leave without a family portrait holding balloons' when he called out to his parents, "*Sourire a' la camera*... smile for the camera!"

At dawn, Mrs. Claudette Choo surprised him, decorating the train cabin with a string of paper hearts.

"A reminder you are so loved, a chain of lasting memories," she shared with Jon-Claude Philippe Choo, before he leaves Paris for the big tent of America.

"*Merci*, I won't forget," he replied.

At 7am, Jon-Claude departs. Kissing them both on the cheek, he bravely gets into a yellow taxi.

"Hello there sir, transporting an aquatic animal will cost you more," the driver declared, adding ten cents to the fare.

"Absolutely! My old man taught me that trick, what's fair is fair. Besides, she goes with me when I leave the tracks - with her, I don't look back."

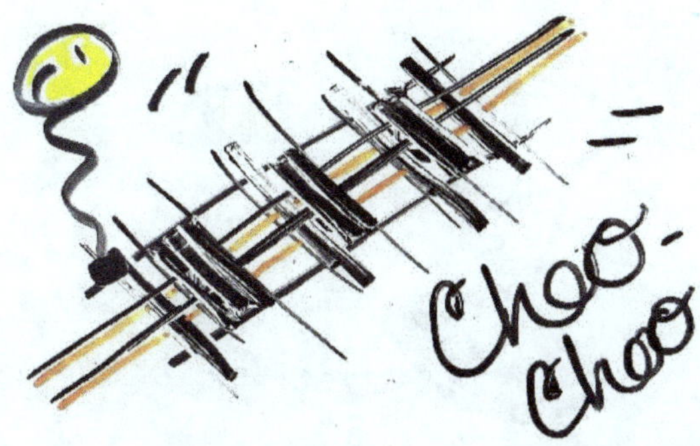

Onboard the plane, Jon-Claude wrote a note... and read it to his fish:

Life is like a balloon... I learned too soon. Sometimes inflated, sometimes deflated. All you ever need is shelter, oxygen, water, food, and a best friend like you.

P.S. I'm glad you're with me, Pinky le' Poo - a bit too often, just kidding.

"Alright, stop all the mushy fried bologna your spatting," Pinky wished to say in return.

Flying was a challenge especially, her demanding attitude. Neither up, nor down, although steady and always there for him.

"Please stop banging on the cup; we have 24hrs at this altitude," said Jon-Claude, hoping for good luck.

Together they flew, to famous NYC American Clown School.

Upon landing, he painted his shoes for the first day – putting one left foot in front of the other, when his phone rang...

“Hi honey, don’t be shy. You learned how to ride a tricycle not to fall, so be brave like back in the day and run along. Immerse yourself fully in activities, not to miss out on festivities,” said Mrs. Claudette Choo.

“Surely, will do, *mere*.”

“Please, *S’il vous plait,* dear.”

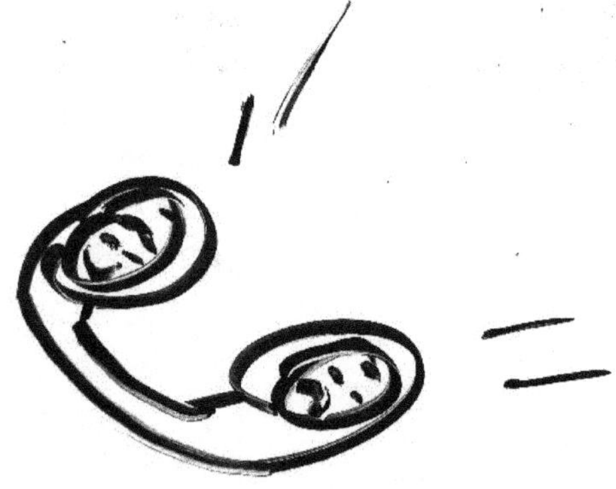

Driving through the city streets, missing home, he noticed a couple kissing next to an alley cat, closely hissing at a fat rat. Knowing then, a new life awaits him.

Stepping into the historic classroom with crackling wooden floors and bricked walls, the teacher Miss Amelia handed out colorful name tags to welcome all.

"*Bienvenue,* welcome today" is written on the chalkboard. As with, "Thank you for attending and don't forget to wear your masks if you want to pass this class," she tells them, "and turn your frowns upside down. Let's introduce ourselves and be proud other's bond - gossiping about you."

In the room, sits a group of students who appear to be extremely bored, whilst the other's snored. Overtime, they transformed into happy, wacky, totally la-dee-da - class-clowns.

Miss. Amelia, a friendly mime in her free time, has another refreshing idea in mind. An adventure full of aroma from fresh petals to vine ripe fruits at the neighborly farmer's market. A field trip to boot.

Walking through the isles absolutely delighted, imposter friend Clown Jules, is standing with a peculiar stare, who obnoxiously burped.

“Smell that?! Bahaha,” he said with a smirk.

“Disgusting!” shouted his longtime pal, Clown Jubilee, squirting him with a fake flower.

Chasing each other, they knocked over a barrel of tangerines and oranges.

"Whoops, a teachable moment; we will learn to juggle, you'll thank me later," said Miss Amelia. "Do you mind, sir?"

"Not at all' give it a whirl," replied the man who owns the produce, now on the floor.

Forming a circle, the clowns tossed fruits dropping them repeatedly, when realizing this is reality, nothing is perfect.

Another stop on the field trip, Little Paris Park. A young lady in a chiffon dress with a scarf around her neck drew caricatures inside hearts; Jon-Claude kept looking back.

"Hey you," she blurted aloud, "can I draw you, no charge."

Turning around, he mutters, "What in the New York hale?! I'm not for sale. Fine, I guess for you, you can."

Looking in her grey eyes, he wonders... does her ring change colors with her mood.'

Friends, who are there waiting for him, ran over to babble, "*Madam*, did you know his Grandpa built the *Rue de Paris!*?"

"*Excusez-moi*? What did you say?" she asked.

The giant 200 ft. wheel he built. Did I stutter?"

"Hmm, you two seem like trouble. Sit down, all three of you; please allow me to draw you unruly bunch of clowns."

"Lady, you are too witty for this trickster, tootles!" They reply intimidated.

Jon-Claude is left with only a pickup line.

The sophisticated young woman did not allow others to ruin her day. Rather annoyed, she went on to sketch the men's mysterious faces anyway. Pictured in mellow-yellow hearts, they began to look distorted; Jon-Claude's cheeks turn bright red.

"What is your name?" he asked blushing.

"Penelope, what about you?"

"Stunning like you," he said. "May I ask for your number?"

She took a risk and exchanged digits.

Later he called to say, "I don't have much, but I would love to spoil you."

At nine o'clock pm, they met at the park, where Penelope waits in the dark - doodling the moon on a cocktail napkin.

"There you are, like a shining star. A true beauty."

"Hello handsome, shall we?" she gestured, while collecting her belongings.

Hugging him tightly, they strolled to a speakeasy where served: *hor's d oeuvers*, *potato a' graten*, a *pate'* and for dessert – the magnificent, torched *crème brulee*.

"So, Penelope, *poly vu France*'? Did I hear you speak it earlier?"

"*Oui*," she replied, "yes, I do."

"No way. You speak French, my parents will love you! It's almost too good to be true."

"It may just be *mon bijou*. Only time will tell, my jewel."

Now young adults, they dined as he leaned over to whisper, "More *Monet* for you?"

"The vine or the canvas?" she asks, accompanied by a glass of the finest.

"The vine my love. It will grow for you."

"Proof is in the pudding, Mr. Choo," she clarified, ending the night with a curtsy or two.

That eve with different clocks and schedules, he telephoned his mother, who advised, “Be wise, the roots of your blooms are what matter.” “Thanks mom,” he answered, placing the phone down to consult Pinky le’ Poo.

Waving at his aquarium, he asked his pet, “Hey Pinky, are you awake?”

“Well, what took you so long; I’m lonely here watching awful re-runs,” replied the fish in bubbles, “and open the darn curtains. Please move the shades; more light is needed or else I’ll fade,” requesting a bigger habitat.

"Your wish is my promise; you would have made a perfect clown fish," he joked, "sorry, did I say that aloud..."

"Enough of the funny business. Have you met someone, goofy?" signaled Pinky le' Poo.

"Yes, a lady of couture, who I adore."

"So, will I be - third wheel party-pooper?"

"Not exactly... most likely... possibly, you will - be where we are," Jon-Claude replied.

"I can live with that if you can't live without her; just always remember to change my water."

Over the years, Jon-Claude Phillipe Choo and Penelope dated through high school and clown university.

At home, unbelievably outliving himself, Pinky congratulates him, "Way to go homie, you did it fool, graduated valedictorian of clown-school!"

Pals, Clown Jules and Jubilee, had an idea to get them off their feet, to start a small circus in Central Park, New York.

Penelope joined too, purchasing a yellow truck filled to the brim with glitzy costumes, disposable cameras, and a helium machine. A present she donated from life savings.

Low on funds, he called his childhood buddy, Mr. Carnie Cahoots, who sells county favorites' candied cashews. Luckily, it was out of season; with nothing better to do, he packed a portable stand and headed there with friends.

Birds chirped; the sunshine bright, as the show began. Hopeful, cheerful, optimistic.

"Over here! Get some cashews, cause life is full of nuts!" shouts the towns newest clown to give a hoot, Mr. Cahoots.

Ignorance was bliss, when doing cartwheels and entertaining alongside, portrait art.

Then suddenly, Jon-Claude Phillipe Choo lost balance and ate dirt.

“Are you okay; were you dropped on your head as a toddler?” asked Clown Jules showcasing a ridiculous foiled crown.

“No, I slipped! They never showed you that trick?” he asked slumping forward, muddy and making moves.

“It’s okay, if you want to be a wacky doo,” said Clown Jubilee, “it adds character.”

“Glad you approve,” thinking to himself, “as if anyone’s opinion is worth two cents.”

Just then, an elegant woman dressed in red with a head of flowers and a tall man sat at Penelope's booth, sharing, "Hello mam, a humble woman to paint free for those in need."

It was recognizable; a voice that was heard since birth. Jon-Claude Phillipe Choo turned around to notice his parents in town.

"*Mere, Pere*, you're here!? What a surprise!"

"Yes dear, a man you've become, we're so proud of you. If not too busy, we would like to treat you and your gal to an enchanting dinner, then a ferry ride."

Mr. and Mrs. Choo have concerns for the flirtatious pair, "May I ask you a question in case you fall in love with my adorable, imbecile son."

"Absolutely, it's understandable, she replied."

"Are you an introvert, extrovert or half and half clown?" asked Mrs. Claudette Choo

"Hmm, according to the playbooks, they have the same outcome - to spontaneously meet your maker," she answered.

"We don't want to miss out on life, ha-ha," his mother replied, finding humor in common.

Jon-Claude realizes she is the one.

"But seriously, how did he win the fish he takes everywhere with us?" Penelope asked in return, considering it a bad habit.

"I told him... get this done, or it can't be won. A game not for the lame, and he did it."

"A winner. I too, love the topic of philosophy," Penelope answers looking at him, sipping, a glass of mixed red and white vino.

Mr. Claude intrigued, dare ask, "*Madam*, may I know how you value your art?"

"Easy. What would one have to pay you - to spit on it, to tear it apart, to smash it in front of you? That's its worth."

"Where did you ever learn to speak like that?" Mr. Claude then asked in shock.

"New York, of course. It goes together... art, and a classic dirty mouth."

"Alrighty, so' ahh... bread and escargot anyone?" Mrs. Claudette interrupted, cutting the tension with a knife.

Afterward, they went for a short ride to view the Statue of Liberty when time to say goodbye had arrived quickly. .

"I hope you will visit soon," Mrs. Claudette said before departing to the city of Paris.

Life was a party, seemingly, until funds drained him unclean.

"Just think, it could be worse with only a penny in your shoe," said Clown Cahoots, playing the kazoo.

"You're right!" agreed Jon-Claude, suggesting a new and improved act was needed. "I know how to perform. I know what to do. A bigger circus we will call - Cirque Soile of America," he said.

The crew stuck together like glue, then bounced off one another like rubber. They landed on the local news, grabbing Ms. Amelia's attention. In a few days' time, a mime was included to bring in more profit. Eventually, collectively, renting an apartment.

Part Four:

The Last Show

Life was swell, until disaster struck, causing an unthinkable train wreck proving happiness does not maneuver in a straight line. Thankfully, the lease was up.

Jon-Claude would receive a *par avion* – airmail that said, "Our deepest regrets, but your parents are dead. I hope you're okay. Please call us, they left you an inheritance, don't hesitate."

There, he stood still in tacky attire when tragedy occurred; his world shattered. In a teal suit with gold pin stripes, painted lashes, puffy hair, and a black top hat - he looked to his best friend.

"Now what happens..." he asked Pinky le' Poo, "is this where it all falls apart?"

"You know, my love," said Penelope, " you really shouldn't give up. I have something to tell you... there's a blessing inside of me, I share with you."

“Are you serious. Now is not the time to clown around, he replied with a sigh.

“Yes, it’s true. A little me and you.”

“Well, I guess the next thing to do, is to buy an airstream for a bigger homestead.”

Unsure of their future amidst thunder, they board the plane with paint in one hand and faith in the other, unbothered by turbulence. Together, they doodle a picture of love in a heart without blunder, and a tribute that read...

Carnival in Paris

"To my beloved parents,

This little light of mine...I'm going to let it shine...

Until we meet again in heaven,

Words can't express how much more than a dozen balloons you meant to me.

An inspiration in life to stay on track.

A kind smile to those who struggle.

A meal for the less fortunate.

An educator to a child, and a heart for animals.

Persons who would never forget a birthday gift, or after-school snack.

The ones I called and talked to for hours.

Just like this poem could go on, words will never explain fully what I want to say.

A calmness surrounds me when I think of you.

Throughout my day, I know angels exist.

Having you in my life made it complete.

Je vous aime'... I love you."

Fashionably late, the rest of the crew arrived too lightening the mood, as they continued the day. In town, Penelope was busy. While she was away shopping, Jon-Claude Phillipe Choo had a trick up his sleeve, something unlikely - a mirrored home with a huge red bow. Inside, a bouquet of roses and a dozen balloons tied to a glossy black Steinway Piano that awaited her.

“Surprise!” shouted the clowns of Cirque Soile, from the back of a dumpy pick-up truck.

Walking in the door feeling grand ore, she said, “Wow, the style is, um... demure, sophisticated, and couture.”

“I want to give you the world sweetheart.”

“We shall see, sweetie...” she replied.

The following weeks, Jon-Claude Phillipe Choo had only one priority; to keep his promise and impress Penelope, who carry his growing baby.

That evening, they strolled to a beautiful historic theater for a moment of photography; a perfect scenery before taking a shortcut down Loop Road to the *Avenue de' le Opera St*.

On the way, feeling hangry.

“Forget the fancy food. Anything to make a turd will do,” Jon-Claude Phillipe Choo insisted.

“So, your saying you want a glitzy hotdog-baby? Is that what I heard?” she asked.

“*Cest la vie, honey*!” he replied. “That’s life.”

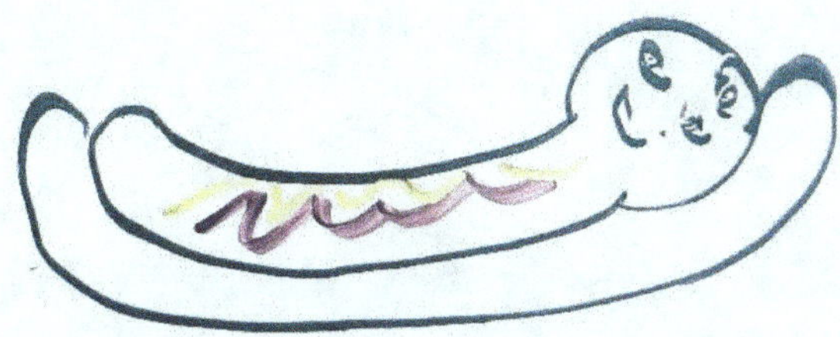

Feeling a bit bamboozled, unexpectedly, a new chapter began. That night, he made plans for his date taking no chances on disrupting his fate, he shared, “You are the caramel apple of my eye...”
They strive daily to stay alive, asking each other, “I wonder where we’ll be in 2025?”
Matchy-matchy carnie’s, Yuti and Tuti blurted aloud, “I hope for our sake, all of your dreams come true or we are broke, bahaha!”

Lying awake, he decided life is too short to be depressed. Instead of moping, he will propose not to end up just a carcass - bag of bones. Consulting the fluorescent fish about family, he said, “I died a little inside, yet they still seem very much alive until the end of time, like a strange phenomenon.”

“Right, to never leave the fun house… ha, a wishful dream. It will be fine, tomorrow’s a new day,” said Pinky le’ Poo.

“Thanks bestie, we must return to Paris to bury my parents. I won’t throw them in a furnace if I can help it.”

Jon-Claude Phillipe Choo had to regulate his emotions to be a better version of himself before falling into despair, unsure if Penelope would accompany him. The destiny of Cirque Soile' of America was now an unsettling truth.

"Don't let her get away, put a ring on it," advised Pinky le' Poo with vague memory.

Having more courage than a lion he once knew, he bowed his knee in humility and asked his girlfriend, "Will you be my forever goof?"

On a quiet night in December, they wed under a sparkling tower of lights. Beneath, a reflective full moon and galaxy of stars.

The honeymoon, celebrated at *Le Grau-du-Roi*, where they purchased a wooden baby carriage with giant wheels. Eventually, returning to the sanctuary zoo with their newborn baby in Paris.

Four months later, by the flattened copper coin machine, Penelope sneezes aahh aah cheuuww... giving birth to an unusual baby girl with eleven toes. Appropriately naming her - Penny Novelty Choo.

In celebration, Jon-Claude Phillipe Choo tosses her up to the heavens with arms stretched wide. Overjoyed, he counted, "One-two-three, *un-du-twa.*" Catching Penny, with a kiss on the cheek.

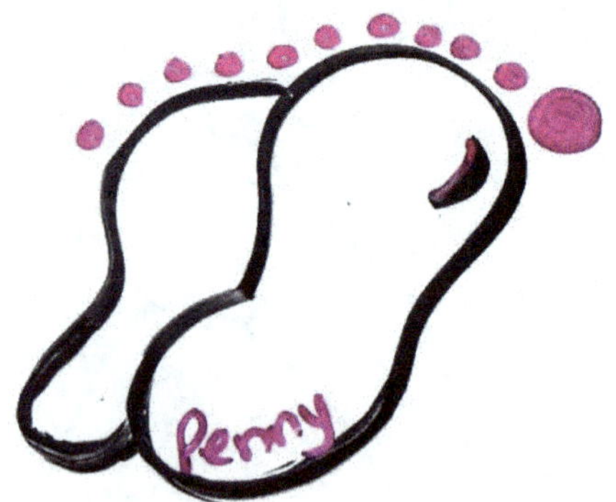

"Well, well, *excusez-moi*, sir do we need another admission?" asked the zookeeper.

"Um, hi, what is your name?" Inquired the new father.

"Mr. Babsy, what's it to you?"

"Well, Mr. Babsy, we seem to have an issue with a bit of a situation, my wife just had a baby. May we purchase one more ticket?"

"No, it's on me, totally free. I insist," the zookeeper replied handing him a ticket, adding, "with a rare name as hers, she'll be royalty here." Then said, "Admit one."

Penny Novelty Choo received a year pass to the local zoo, having the last laugh.

Spectators walked away as they shouted, "*Ovua!* Goodbye, for now. Best wishes to you."

The End

DRAW THE CLOWNS

Author's Bio

A passion for Fine Arts at an early age participating in theater. Love for the theatrics continued over the years when attending performing arts, musicals, and a variety of performances. Traveling has been an inspiration in life. Art never faded, working on many crafty projects. Eventually, discovering a desire to write after receiving a 'literary vision' inspiring to write a book about helping animals, earthlings, and planet-home. See Author's Page for upcoming book releases and dates.

www.ingramcontent.com/pod-product-compliance
Lightning Source LLC
LaVergne TN
LVHW010617110826
845149LV00003B/944

* 9 7 9 8 9 9 2 5 1 9 9 6 9 *